DISCOVERY
ON THE
DUORO

RIVER CRUISE
COZIES
BOOK FOUR

CHERYL DOUGAN

DISCOVERY ON THE DUORO

A RIVER CRUISING COZY MYSTERY

CHERYL DOUGAN

DOUGAN PRESS

DOUGAN PRESS

CONTENTS

1. Porto   1
Discover the New World

2. Regua   25
Don't Break the Dishes

3. Castelo Rodrigo   39
Everything in Moderation, Including Moderation.

4. Salamanca   45
Where is Waldo?

5. Favaios   59
Go Comb Monkeys

6. Lamego   71
Everyone Should Do What They Do Best

7. Porto   77
A Second Chance

Join the Newsletter   93

Good Karma   95

Also by Cheryl Dougan   97

About the Author   99

CHAPTER 1
PORTO
DISCOVER THE NEW WORLD

Adelle watched silently as Barb strode to the bed closest to the sliding balcony door, picked up Adelle's carry-on luggage, and moved it to the other single bed in their cabin. "I get the bed by the window," she said.

"Why?" Adelle was disappointed. She had been looking forward to gazing out at the river, enjoying the moonlit nights and early morning sunrises from the comfort of her bed.

"You're as old as my mother, and she's always up several times a night," Barb replied.

Adelle briefly debated arguing with Barb, but she knew it was a waste of energy. Once Barb's mind was made up about something, there was no changing it.

As Adelle hung up her clothes, she got distracted by their view. Their river cruise ship was docked in Vila Nova de Gaia on the south side of the Duoro River. The white buildings with red roofs on the hills of Porto across the river shimmered in the mid-day sun. After spending two days in Lisbon, then traveling to Porto that day by motorcoach, she was eager to river cruise with her girlfriends again.

"Why do you need so many outfits?" Adelle asked as Barb unpacked her two large suitcases. Traveling with only carry-on was so much simpler. It eliminated a lot of decision-making, and Adelle was tired of making decisions. She was looking forward to relaxing.

"Disguises," Barb answered.

Yes! Adelle thought, pulse racing.

Barely restraining her impatience, Adelle waited for Barb to reveal more.

"What disguises do you think you will need on this trip?" Adelle finally asked.

"Business clothes for client interviews and casual outfits for meals in the ship's restaurant." Barb pointed to her bed and the small counter and chair. "And comfortable clothes for my office." She took an old ragged sweatshirt out of her suitcase and reverently placed it on her bed.

Adelle's mind was in high gear. On the way to Porto, Barb had revealed that she had started her own insurance fraud investigation company. Now it was clear that Barb was working on a case, and Adelle wanted to be involved. She looked at her carry-on, mentally inventorying the few clothes she had packed. Would they be versatile enough? More importantly, how could she contribute to the investigation?

Think, Adelle.

"What about disguises to blend in with the locals?" Adelle asked.

Barb studied Adelle with pursed lips.

"Perhaps Debbie could help you with that," Adelle tentatively suggested.

Barb stared at her.

Uh-oh…

Adelle worried that she had overstepped her bounds until Barb broke out in a wide grin. "Good idea," she said. "You passed your first test. Now for the second one."

Adelle felt proud of herself. She was sure the next test would involve her intelligence, people skills, or …

"It's time to fetch my first coffee."

Strolling through Porto's Old Quarter, Adelle tried to relax. Barb could be exasperating. After delivering her coffee, one-third regular, two-thirds decaf, and lots of hot milk, thus passing the "coffee test," Barb had shooed her out of their shared cabin. She didn't have time for the Porto walking tour. She needed the time to work on her laptop.

Adelle followed the sound of joyful laughter until she saw her friend Debbie walking ahead with another couple. Tilly was trailing behind by herself.

"Look at my little sister," Tilly said, motioning at Debbie. "She's already met half the passengers."

Little sister? Adelle laughed to herself. Debbie was

twelve years younger than Tilly, who was in her seventies, but she was far from little. To use Tilly's expression, she was even more *full-figured* than on their last cruise together. Even her curly blonde hair seemed volumes thicker. Tilly, on the other hand, was still trim and petite with short white hair. Unlike her extroverted sibling, she always seemed quite content to be by herself while Debbie *cavorted* with the other passengers.

"Where's Barb?" Debbie asked as she dropped back to walk with them.

"Working on her laptop," Adelle replied, still smarting from the demeaning coffee task.

"That girl doesn't know how to relax," Tilly said.

"Hello, Pot," Debbie said, chuckling. "What are you working on this trip, Sis?"

Tilly pulled a skein of green and white variegated yarn out of the pocket of her cargo pants. "Blankets for newborns," she said.

Adelle wasn't surprised that Tilly was working on another craft. She preferred to use her time wisely. She was always working on a project while she traveled. Tilly had made fidget quilts on their first river cruise together, from Budapest to Amsterdam. When they sailed from Lyon to Avignon on their second river cruise, Tilly knitted comfort dolls. On their last cruise along the Moselle and Rhine rivers, she made tiny quilts to accompany the comfort dolls.

Debbie smiled. "Are you making granny squares like mom taught us?" she asked.

"Yes," Tilly replied, pulling a finished square out of another pant pocket. She handed it to Debbie. "I hope you remember how to crochet," Tilly said. "I'm going to need some help this trip." She looked expectantly at Adelle. "It's pretty easy, Adelle. Even you should be able to crochet squares."

"I'm too old to learn a new craft," Adelle said.

"Nonsense," Tilly said. "I'll teach you. After all, you know what they say."

"What?" Adelle asked. Tilly was a fountain of homespun wisdom.

"We don't stop learning because we get old," Tilly said. "We get old because we stop learning."

So true, Adelle thought. She loved Tilly's practical prairie wisdom and was grateful for the opportunity to travel with the sisters again. After floundering in retirement, Adelle had been dreadfully bored until her first stint as a river cruise tour host when she met "the girls": Barb, Debbie, Tilly, and Teresa. Her life had been full of the promise of travel and adventure ever since.

This trip promised to be even more exciting. At the end of their last trip, Barb had hinted that she was going to start her own fraud investigation business. With associates! Every day since, Adelle had been dreaming about the possibilities. She wanted to be an associate and help Barb with her investigations. She knew she had more to offer than barista skills.

Set on the hillside overlooking the Duoro River, the medieval old city of Porto, called the Ribeira district, was charming. Following their local guide, Adelle felt like she was taking a step back in time. Strolling past the colorful buildings on the waterfront and up through the narrow winding streets above, she wondered how many generations had lived and worked there over the centuries.

"Too bad Teresa couldn't join us," Tilly said when their guide mentioned that they were in the middle of a UNESCO World Heritage site. "She could have checked another site off her list."

Debbie giggled. "I'm sure she would rather be on her honeymoon than with us."

Adelle agreed. After their last cruise, Teresa met the owner of a large wholesale business. "It was love at first sight," she had exclaimed when she had contacted Adelle to explain why she had canceled her trip to Portugal. Adelle sighed contentedly. She knew the feeling. The same thing had happened to her all those years ago when she first met Wes. Sometimes she felt like they were still honeymooning. Once again, she was grateful he had encouraged her to travel with the girls while he helped out on his friend's farm.

Standing in the shadow of the beautiful and historic Porto Cathedral, their guide pointed out the house where Henry the Navigator was born in 1394. He said there were many monuments around Portugal honoring the Portuguese explorer, soldier, and prince. Henry the Navigator had sent many expeditions from Portugal to the west coast of Africa and was credited with establishing a center studying navigation, naval architecture, and astronomy, leading to the development of a powerful ship called a caravel.

"We are very proud of our Golden Age of Discovery when Portuguese caravels set sail in search of new worlds," the guide said. As he listed Portugal's maritime achievements, Adelle was lost in thought. She tried to imagine what it was like to be a sailor, believing the world was flat and yet willing to leave home despite the risk of sailing off the edge of the ocean into the dark unknown.

"Earth to Adelle," Debbie whispered, pulling her aside. "I need your help this trip." Debbie had never looked so serious. "Something is bothering Tilly, but she won't say anything. I thought you might be able to discover what it is."

That was odd, Adelle thought. The sisters shared everything together. Before she could find out more information, Tilly headed in their direction. "I'll try," she whispered.

The next stop on the tour was the Sao Bento train station, another UNESCO World Heritage Site and national monument of Portugal, which opened to the public in 1916. It had to be one of the most beautiful train stations in the world. Gazing around the vestibule with the high ceiling, Adelle was amazed by the murals depicted in the blue and white tiles. "These glazed ceramic tiles are called *azulejo* tiles," the guide informed them. "There are 20,000 tiles in the station. You will see many more all over Portugal."

The train station was very busy, with passengers scurrying past amidst the echoing announcements of the arriving and departing trains. While Debbie was busy taking pictures of the various historical scenes on the walls, Adelle noticed Tilly standing transfixed in front of one of the central panels. It depicted four agricultural scenes: the vineyards, the harvest, the wine shipment down the Duoro River, and work in a watermill. "You don't see this back home," Tilly said in awe. *That's for sure*, thought Adelle. Tilly lived in Saskatchewan on the same farm where she was born. The setting couldn't be more different; rolling hills with terraces of grapevines versus flat rows of cereal grains.

After exploring the train station, their guide led them to Rua da Flores, "the flower street," which had been in that location since 1521. Recently renovated, it was now one of the trendiest streets in Porto and the perfect spot for some free time.

"You two can sit and have coffee while I shop for Barb," Debbie had suggested. She was in her element. Barb had texted her, asking if she could buy her a traditional Portuguese scarf. Debbie loved to shop, and she was only too happy to help.

Adelle was relieved that she didn't have to shop. Instead, she could use the opportunity to chat privately with Tilly. As they waited for their café au lait, Tilly fished a small notebook and pencil out of yet another pant pocket.

"Are you collecting trivia notes?" Adelle asked. On their previous cruise, Tilly had been determined to win the nightly contests in the lounge.

"No," Tilly said. "This trip, I am going to rely on my memory for trivia facts and figures. It's good for the brain." She flipped her notebook open and wrote a short note. "I'm jotting down ideas to take home with me," she explained before putting the notebook away. "Do you remember my park?" Tilly asked.

Adelle recalled the park with a smile. Tilly and her girlfriends had transformed a vacant lot in the small town near Tilly's farm into a community gathering place.

"The town administrators liked what we did so well that they've encouraged my friends and me to enter a provincial contest. We're competing with other small towns to see who has the most beautiful town."

"Did you see something of interest here?" Adelle asked.

"We have an old abandoned train station at the end of Main Street that could use a facelift," Tilly replied. "Maybe we can have some murals painted on it."

"Who pays for your projects?" Adelle asked.

Tilly sighed. "We have access to some grants, but we also need to fundraise. So, I need to come up with ideas."

So that's what is bugging Tilly, Adelle realized. Half the solution to a problem was knowing what the problem was. But why wasn't Tilly talking to Debbie about fundraising? They talked about everything and everyone else. The sisters were the queens of gossip. Adelle had finally accepted that fact. After all, she wasn't immune to the odd bit of gossip herself. However, she tried not to share any news unless it affected her firsthand. That way, she didn't worry so much. There was too much stress she couldn't avoid without avoiding the stress she could. She tried to pretend that whoever she was talking about could hear what she was saying. It made life so much simpler.

You still haven't answered your question, Adelle. Why doesn't Tilly want to confide in Debbie?

It was a mystery.

Barb joined Adelle and the sisters as the servers circulated throughout the ship's lounge, passing out glasses of port before dinner.

"I found a scarf for you," Debbie said, unfolding a black rectangular scarf with fringes and a colorful floral pattern. Debbie showed her how to drape it around her shoulders like the locals. "When in Rome, wear what the Romans wear," she said.

The program director began the welcome aboard introduction. She introduced herself as Amelia, a name that meant "brave" and "diligent" in her native Portuguese language. Then she introduced some of her fellow staff members, including the maître d' and the chef. "They're the most important staff," she said, winking as she nodded at the ship's captain standing on her left. Adelle liked her already! She would fit right in with the girls.

Amelia raised her glass in a Portuguese toast. "*Saude*."

"When in Porto, Portugal, drink port like the Portuguese do," Debbie quipped, joining in the toast.

"Try saying that five times fast," Adelle suggested.

"Good idea." Debbie whipped out her phone. "You can video Tilly and me."

The sisters only got through the phrase twice before they started to giggle as Adelle videoed them. Adelle joined in, laughing at how surprised Debbie would be later when she edited the hundreds of pictures and videos she would no doubt be recording on their trip. Before Adelle pressed stop, Tilly had made a silly face and stuck out her tongue.

"Tonight, we are docked in Vila Nova de Gaia across the river from Porto," Amelia continued. "We will leave tomorrow morning. For the next eight days, we are going to sail the Duoro River. Unlike other river cruises you may have been on, we only sail during the day. You'll be able to take in all the beautiful scenery as we make our way to various villages and wineries. In the evenings, feel free to explore on your own."

Adelle was lost in memories of previous excursions with the girls when Barb poked her in the ribs. "Pay attention," she said, gesturing at Amelia. "She's talking about port."

"Wine has been produced by traditional landholders in the Duoro region for some two thousand years,"

Amelia said. "Throughout the centuries, row upon row of terraces have been built according to different techniques." Amelia raised her glass of port and studied it appreciatively. "Since the eighteenth century, the Duoro region's main product has been port wine."

Adelle was surprised to learn that port was rumored to be a British creation as much as a Portuguese one. Britain had traditionally imported wine from France, but during the wars with France in the seventeenth and eighteenth centuries, Britain had boycotted French wine and looked elsewhere.

"Portuguese wine often didn't survive the long sea journey to England," Amelia said. "It is rumored that the port-making process was invented accidentally by a pair of brothers when they fortified the wine with brandy in order to maintain its quality during the long trip."

"That explains a lot," Debbie whispered. "Our British grandmother used to fortify herself each evening with a nip of brandy."

"For medicinal reasons," Tilly added, raising her glass in a mock toast before taking another sip.

Debbie winked as she smiled at her sister. "The apple didn't fall far from the tree."

As they left the lounge to go for dinner in the ship's restaurant, Barb quietly asked Adelle what she knew about port.

"Nothing," Adelle admitted.

Barb pursed her lips. "If you're going to work with me, you better be a quick learner."

Dinner that night featured Portuguese specialties. Adelle couldn't make up her mind as she stared at the menu. Should she order the *Picanha Com Esmagado de Batata e Espinafres*, translated underneath as seared rump steak with crushed potatoes? Or *Caldeirada*, Portuguese fish and seafood stew? All she knew for sure was that she didn't want what Barb had ordered - hamburger and fries from the 'Classic Menu' selection.

"Where's your sense of adventure?" Adelle teased, still tingling with excitement about possibly working with Barb.

"Food is fuel," Barb answered.

Adelle shook her head. Some of her girlfriends' husbands were like that back home. They raced through every meal, eager to leave the table and go back to whatever they were doing. They didn't even stay for dessert!

Which reminded her of the delicious desserts on her previous cruises. She quickly scanned the bottom of her menu. *Quindim de Coco com Ananás*, caramelized pineapple and coconut cake. Her mouth watered. Wes loved coconut. She wondered what he was having for dinner. Likely roast beef sandwiches and coffee while sitting on the tailback of his half-ton, taking a "fuel" break in the field while helping his friend at the farm.

"I'm having fish," Tilly said. "It's good for your brain."

Finally, Adelle made her decision. She chose the

fish to fuel her mind. Afterward, she could eat cake to fuel her sugar cravings.

"I've researched our itinerary," Tilly said, handing the menu back to their server. "We are going to visit several UNESCO sites this week."

"Too bad Teresa isn't here," Barb said.

"That's what Tilly said," Debbie told Barb. Her eyes twinkled. "I guess you and Adelle are back to sharing a cabin again. How's that going so far?"

Barb raised one eyebrow and smirked. "Interesting."

Uh-oh …

Much to Adelle's chagrin, Barb told the sisters what had happened when she had momentarily closed the drapes while Adelle was putting her empty carry-on bag under her bed.

"I wanted to test the backlight setting for my laptop screen," Barb explained.

"You should have warned me," Adelle said. "All of a sudden, our room was pitch black."

Barb snickered. "Then I turned my cellphone flashlight on."

"When my back was turned," Adelle added.

"She jumped straight in the air."

"At her own shadow?" Debbie asked.

"Affirmative."

Adelle's stomach fluttered again just thinking about it. When her startle reflex kicked in, she had indeed flinched at her own shadow, which had caused her to jump yet again.

As the girls laughed, Adelle finally found the humor

in the situation. Soon she was laughing along with them. It was great to be together again.

"Are you working on a case?" Debbie asked Barb as their server handed back their menus to choose dessert.

"Affirmative."

"What are you investigating?" Tilly asked.

Adelle put her menu down. She was curious, too.

Before Barb could say anything, her phone pinged. Barb read the screen, took a selfie, sent a short text, and then stood up from the table. "Business," she explained. "I'll tell you later." She made brief eye contact with Adelle, then left.

"What's with the selfie?" Tilly asked.

"Probably just checking her hair," Debbie replied. "I do it all the time."

Tilly rolled her eyes. "Adelle, do you know what she's working on?"

Adelle paused before answering. On their last cruise, she had learned the hard way that honesty was the best policy. And she could honestly say that she didn't have a clue what Barb was working on. "Not yet."

Adelle and the sisters lingered over coffee and dessert, catching up on their lives since their last trip together. Debbie's new café in her clothing consignment store was thriving. "Remember those smiling angel ornaments I bought on our last cruise?" Debbie asked. "I gave them as gifts to some of my less fortunate customers." She clapped her hands together in delight. "They love them! I'm looking forward to more shopping on this trip."

The sisters laughed when Adelle wrinkled her nose. They knew that shopping was her least favorite activity.

"What have you done about your kitchen since we last saw you?" Tilly asked.

Adelle told the sisters that she and Wes had compromised on updating their house. Wes had agreed to paint the kitchen walls, and when Adelle had seen how much brighter the room looked, she was content to leave the oak cabinets as they were. However, the fresh paint revealed how shabby the flooring was. One thing had led to another, and they had just completed a full renovation. She was tired of making decisions. Who knew there were that many shades of taupe?

Their conversation turned to Tilly. She was cautiously optimistic that the crops would yield well. "Unless it doesn't rain, or it does, and we get hailed out." Adelle shook her head. She couldn't understand farmers. Their entire livelihood depended on things that were totally out of their control. It was too much risk for her. She found herself thinking about Henry the Navigator again. When she jokingly referred to Tilly as Tilly the Cultivator, she knew it was time for bed.

Standing in front of her cabin door, Adelle summoned the courage to be like Debbie and ask Barb what she was working on. She wanted to know what she could do to help. Taking a deep breath and squaring her shoulders, Adelle opened the door.

The room was pitch black. As the door closed behind her, Adelle reached her arms out in search of her bed. She didn't want to wake Barb up.

Ouch!

Adelle bashed her knee, then jumped backward.

Breathe, Adelle, breathe.

Calming down, she backed up and fumbled around until she found the light switch.

You were attacked by a chair.

Rubbing her knee, Adelle slowly registered that Barb wasn't there. Her bed hadn't been disturbed. The chair had been placed between the door and Adelle's bed. She saw her cellphone and a handwritten note on the seat of the offending chair.

"*Tried to text you,*" Barb had written, followed by a large arrow pointing to Adelle's phone.

"*Couldn't wait any longer,*" was scrawled under the arrow.

Uh-oh…

When Barb had left the dinner table earlier, was Adelle supposed to go with her? Before dessert was served?

Setting the chair back where it belonged, Adelle wondered where Barb had gone. She wasn't on board. Before returning to the cabin, Adelle had roamed throughout the ship, walking off calories. Why had she boobytrapped their cabin?

To get your attention.

Now what? Adelle opened the drapes and looked out. It was dark and foggy. Adelle shivered. There was no way she was going out there alone.

What if Barb is in trouble?

Adelle started to feel panicky. The poor girl was out there somewhere by herself, and Adelle was supposed to be with her.

Be brave, Adelle. You can do this.

Adelle looked out the window again. How could she find her?

She had an idea. Maybe Amelia knew where Barb had gone.

———

Amelia had confirmed Adelle's suspicion - Barb had asked her for directions to a nearby Port House. Amelia must have sensed Adelle's fear because she had offered to walk the short distance with her.

Adelle grabbed Amelia's arm as they passed small boats next to the boardwalk. There were men crouched on the deck.

"Those aren't men; they are barrels," Amelia said, putting Adelle at ease. The small boats with curved prows were called *rabelos*. "They are the traditional Portuguese wooden cargo boats used to transport goods and people along the Duoro River," Amelia explained. "See how they have a flat bottom? That innovation helped them navigate the shallow, fast-flowing waters of the upper Duoro. Before the arrival of the railway, the *rabelo* was the fastest and most efficient means to transport wine from the Duoro Valley to Porto."

"Do they still use them to ship wine?" Adelle asked.

"Not anymore," Amelia replied wistfully. "In 1968, locks and hydroelectric dams started to be built on the river. The *rabelos* were retired from active service."

When they reached the Port House, Adelle tensed up again. "Do you want to go inside with me?" she asked Amelia.

"Sorry, I have to get back to the ship."

Adelle hesitated.

Amelia patted Adelle's arm. "Do you hear the music inside?"

Adelle could hear the faint sounds of a heartfelt song accompanied by string instruments.

"It's fado music," Amelia explained. "You'll learn more about fado on our cruise."

Adelle watched nervously as Amelia turned and left. She was tempted to follow her back.

Stalling, she stood aside to let a very pregnant young woman enter.

Be brave, Adelle. She took a deep breath and opened the door.

The music was coming from a low stage to the left. Although Adelle couldn't understand the words, she was soon mesmerized by the female vocalist, backed up by young men wearing black suits, playing mandolins and classical guitar.

Ouch!

Adelle jumped when she felt a sharp jab to her right shoulder. Spinning around, she saw Barb gesturing to follow her out the door.

"I see you finally decided to join me," Barb said, standing outside with her hands on her hips. "Why didn't you follow me when I left the dinner table?"

So that's what that look meant, Adelle realized. Should she reply that she wasn't a mind reader? Or that she was focused on dessert?

Career limiting move, Adelle. Think.

"I assumed you wanted me to stay and cover for you."

"Wrong answer," Barb said, turning on her heel. "The first rule of a good investigator is to never assume. It makes an ass out of you and me."

Really? Adelle struggled not to laugh out loud at the old cliché.

As they walked past the *rabelos* in the direction of their ship, Adelle couldn't stand the silence. "What were you doing at the Port House?" Adelle finally asked.

Barb took her time before she answered. "Do you remember our last cruise? When I met with a large insurance company in Zurich?"

How could Adelle forget? Before that meeting, Barb had shown her a draft of her new business card. Barb's name was followed by "and Associates." Adelle had thought of little else since she had returned home.

"We kept in touch," Barb continued. "I had mentioned that our next river cruise was tentatively Portugal." Barb slowed down. "They've hired us to investigate a case here."

Us? Adelle tingled with excitement as she contemplated coming out of retirement and returning to active service in her life.

"I just received the file this afternoon. The insurance company hooked me up with one of their summer interns from this area. He arranged to meet me and you at the Port House tonight."

"Both of us?" Adelle asked.

Barb looked toward the water. "The insurance company seemed concerned about my lack of field experience, so I told them I had knowledgeable associates '*on board*.'"

Clever, thought Adelle.

"But I didn't expect they would send someone else to work with us."

Barb came to a standstill and faced Adelle. "Because of you, I was late. I missed him."

Barb had sat facing the door in the far-right corner, waiting for the intern. In the meantime, a man had joined her at her table. Adelle wasn't surprised. Barb was an attractive young woman. She was wearing her new scarf and had taken the time to apply makeup and style her shoulder-length blonde hair.

"When I saw you come in, I finally had an excuse to leave."

At least you're good for something, Adelle.

Summoning her courage, Adelle asked what the investigation was about.

"The case involves a shipment of port. I need to verify that the claim is valid."

"How will you do that?"

"With my specialized analytical and technology training," Barb said without a trace of modesty.

"How?"

"You wouldn't understand," Barb said, giving her standard answer.

"Give me a chance. Try me."

Too late, Adelle realized that Barb hadn't changed. As she launched into a detailed description of her analytical, financial, and documentary research capabilities, followed by her specialized strategic investigative skills, Adelle struggled not to yawn. Like the *rabelos*, her mind was drifting.

"… and that's what this multi-million-dollar case is all about."

Uh-oh…

Adelle had missed the case summary. She didn't dare ask Barb to repeat it again.

You will have to wing it, Adelle.

Barb's phone pinged. She frowned as she read her text. "It's the intern."

"You can blame me," Adelle said, still feeling bad.

"Another lesson," Barb said, pursing her lips as her thumbs hovered over her phone. "Never make excuses."

As Adelle wished she had listened better and known more about the case, she experienced a brainwave. "If we don't meet with him until we return to Porto in a week, we'll know more about the port business by then, and you can train me as your Associate in the meantime."

"Just what I was going to say," Barb said, finishing

and sending her reply. "I'll have time to review the documentation while we learn more about the industry. The more informed we are, the better questions we'll be able to ask."

Hearing "we," Adelle perked up again.

As they approached the ramp to the ship, Barb stopped walking and turned to Adelle. "Our goal is to make sure that the claim is legit. I can't afford to make any mistakes - this is my big chance to secure future contracts with significant insurance companies."

Adelle, you can't make any more mistakes, either. "What if you find out the claim is not legit?" she asked.

"That's when it gets interesting," Barb replied. "When millions of dollars are at stake, desperate people do desperate things."

Adelle shivered as she realized that investigations could be dangerous. Looking over the water, she thought of the sailors overcoming their fears of the unknown, leaving the Old World to discover the New World. But one thing was clear. Like the explorers, she needed more adventure in her life.

"How can I help?" Adelle asked, following Barb across the ramp of the ship.

"First, you need to start paying closer attention," Barb said. "Until then, you're on probation."

CHAPTER 2
REGUA
DON'T BREAK THE DISHES

Adelle's morning started at sunrise. After delivering coffee and a muffin to Barb in their cabin as instructed, Adelle took her own coffee up to the sundeck soon after the ship left Porto. She sighed contentedly and sipped from her cup as they sailed past picturesque landscapes of terraced vineyards on rolling hills, interspersed with narrow passages through jagged rocks and steep canyons.

"Beautiful, isn't it?"

Adelle turned to see Amelia standing beside her at the railing.

"The Duoro journey is over nine hundred kilometers," she said. "Or five hundred sixty miles, if you prefer."

As there were many Americans, Canadians, Brits, and two couples from Australia on the cruise, Amelia often used both metric and imperial measures.

"The river looks so tame," Adelle observed.

"That's because of the hydroelectric dams I was telling you about. They're on both sides of the border between Portugal and Spain," Amelia explained.

Always curious about people's paths in life, Adelle discovered that Amelia had been born into a family who had been involved in the wine industry for generations.

"The industry has consolidated," Amelia said. "Now it's mostly large companies. But before that, my great grandfather used to pilot *rabelos* down this river, shipping barrels of wine to Porto. These days, it's shipped in tanker trucks." Amelia smiled as she gazed off into the distance. "Thanks to my career, I get to revisit my favorite childhood memories of hearing family stories about shipping port on the Duoro."

As they entered the first of five locks on their cruise, Adelle was impressed as the captain carefully steered the ship into the lock with only a few inches to spare on either side. She was surprised by how much the ship rose. Amelia told her it was the deepest lock in Europe.

"Are you going to the cork presentation in the lounge at ten?" Amelia asked as their ship exited the lock to continue their journey. "You'll have a chance to shop."

Adelle politely replied that she had made other plans. *Like sorting my socks*, her inside voice said as she watched Amelia go.

Over coffee in their cabin earlier, Barb had stressed the need for Adelle to always be observant and aware of what was happening around her. Scanning the deck, she saw Tilly sitting by herself, working on her craft project.

It was a good time to find out why she wouldn't talk to Debbie about her fundraising concern.

Tilly looked up and smiled as Adelle sat down beside her. She fished into the pocket of her cargo pants and handed Adelle yarn and a crochet hook.

Staring at the hook, Adelle remembered a time when her grandmother was visiting. Adelle had just started Girl Guides. She was excited to earn her first craft badge. Her grandmother had tried to teach her how to crochet, but it was hopeless. Hand-to-eye coordination had never been her strength. She didn't get the badge.

Tilly was more determined than Adelle's grandmother.

"Watch. First, stick out your pointer finger and let some yarn dangle from it. Then you make a slip stitch like this," Tilly said, demonstrating how it was done.

As Adelle fumbled with the yarn, Tilly looked around the deck. "Where's Barb? Working?"

Adelle was grateful that she and Barb had discussed what they would tell the sisters. "A good investigator needs to maintain client confidentiality," Barb had insisted. On their previous trip, Adelle had learned the hard way that a good friend needed to maintain honesty. They had agreed to compromise. They would share a minimum amount of information with Tilly and Debbie on a need-to-know basis.

"Yes," Adelle replied truthfully. "Now that she's self-employed, Barb said she would have to spend some of her free time on her laptop."

"There you are," Debbie said as she joined the women on the deck. "Where's Barb?"

"She's making hay," Tilly answered.

"What?" Adelle was puzzled.

"Making hay while the sun shines," Tilly said. "Working while she has the chance." Tilly rolled her eyes. "City girls don't know anything."

Debbie winked as she reached out and took Adelle's yarn and crochet hook. Adelle could have hugged her on the spot. "I've got time to crochet a few squares before the cork presentation," Debbie said.

As they chatted, it was obvious that Tilly had researched their trip. "Portugal is one of the biggest producers of cork in the world," she said. "The cork lady is going to show us products made from local cork trees."

Debbie's fingers were flying. "Amelia said she'll have wallets, small bags, purses, and phone pouches."

Adelle sighed. Shopping wasn't her thing. She could avoid going with the sisters when they were docked. She hadn't anticipated that the shopping would come to them.

"You won't need a phone pouch, Sis, since you forgot your phone."

That's why Tilly was using a notebook again, Adelle realized. On their previous cruises, Barb had patiently shown Tilly how to use a little technology. First, she had taught her how to "Google," not "oogle." Then, on their last trip, Barb showed Tilly how to use her phone to take notes for the trivia contests.

Tilly scowled. "I didn't forget my phone," she huffed. "I simply chose not to bring it."

Good time to change the topic, Adelle.

"This is amazing," Adelle said, picking up the square Debbie had crocheted.

"Thanks," Debbie said as she started another square. "We've started a ladies' craft group in the store's café. I'm always surprised how many young women don't know anything about making crafts."

Adelle wasn't surprised. Not everyone grew up in ideal family circumstances.

"Sis, if it's okay with you, I'm going to take one granny square back with me so that I can show them how to crochet."

Tilly sat up straight and beamed at Debbie. She was obviously pleased. Adelle wished Tilly would look at her like that. Suddenly, she had an inspiration. "Can I join you girls for the cork presentation?"

When Adelle went back to the cabin to freshen up, Barb was working on her laptop. "What have you learned so far?" Barb asked without looking up.

Adelle thought carefully, discarding possible responses as quickly as they surfaced. She couldn't think of anything relevant to the investigation.

"Nothing?" Barb prompted, staring at Adelle.

Shaking her head, Adelle got the hint when she noticed Barb's grin. "What about you?"

"The intern arranged a private tour for us at the second winery this afternoon. He said to look for the employee in the cape."

Cape?

The ship arrived at the town of Regua in midafternoon. Amelia had explained that, unlike other river cruises, many of their daily outings would require a relatively short motorcoach drive from each town to their ultimate destination.

The first excursion was to the Mateus Palace. As they drove up the driveway, Adelle stared at the ornate double stairway leading up to the palace. She had a feeling of déjà vu. She had never been there before, and yet it seemed so familiar.

Debbie laughed as she pointed to the building. "It's the picture on the Mateus wine bottle," she said. "Don't you remember drinking Mateus Rose in your teenage years?"

It all came back to Adelle. She remembered rooming with three other students after she left high school. Mateus Rose bottles had provided the main decor for their apartment. Their green glass and distinctive flask shapes made them perfect containers for flowers and candles.

Debbie had similar memories. "When we were poor newlyweds, we turned the bottles into bases for table lamps," she said.

Their guide told them that the palace had been built in the eighteenth century. As they followed him past priceless furniture and artwork, Adelle was lost in daydreams of her younger years.

The group followed the guide through an extensive library of antique leather-bound books under a high wood-slatted ceiling. She discovered that the ornate wood ceilings were plentiful as they toured the Palace. Wes would love all the chestnut wood on display.

Focus, Adelle.

In the chapel, there was an interesting display of hand-embroidered religious robes. Adelle was pleased to see Tilly talking to another woman about the needle-work. She fervently hoped that Tilly's new friend knew how to crochet.

Outside, Adelle enjoyed free time wandering through the palace's formal gardens. She was impressed by the cedar-lined walkways and the paths through the intricate maze of trimmed low hedges. She made her way down granite steps, under a trellis of red grapes, and into an area surrounded by an assortment of colorful trees, some with silvery leaves that contrasted nicely with the golds and reds of the surrounding foliage.

Nice observation, but not helpful with Barb's case.

Adelle wondered how she could be of value. So far, all she knew was that Barb was investigating a case involving port. Adelle knew nothing about port. How could she possibly help?

"Earth calling Adelle. We need you."

Adelle was ecstatic. Finally, somebody needed her!

Debbie and Tilly were sitting on the retaining wall of the reflecting pool in front of the palace. Debbie held out her phone. "Take our picture with the Palace in the background, please."

"Here," Tilly said, handing her a slice of candied ginger. "You're going to need this."

Adelle was grateful that Tilly was always prepared. She had researched the excursion in advance of their trip, unlike Adelle, who liked to be surprised. The girls all knew of Adelle's problem with motion sickness. Cruising on the river was not a concern; she didn't feel a thing. Driving on winding roads was another issue entirely.

Their driver expertly drove up the narrow switch-back road through the steeply terraced vineyards to the winery perched on top of the mountain. Adelle kept her eyes focused on the back of the seat in front of her. As she fought her nausea, she thought of Wes. Whenever she complained about motion sickness, he responded: "Pumpkin, if that's your biggest problem, you don't have a problem." She knew he was right, but it didn't make her feel any better.

Don't look down, Adelle. Distract yourself.

"Tilly, have you talked to Debbie about fundraising?"

"Let me tell you about the last time I asked her for ideas," Tilly replied. Debbie had suggested a black-tie bingo where participants would dress up in gowns and tuxedos. "She's lived in the city too long," Tilly said, shaking her head. "In small-town Saskatchewan, tuxedos are blue jeans and jean jackets. No one wears gowns anymore. And who wants to play bingo? Borrrring."

Good point. Adelle dropped the topic.

———

Leaving the motorcoach, Adelle made her way to the tour group gathered around the guide. She stood on tiptoe and peeked over the heads in front of her. All she could see was a black flat-rimmed sombrero. Circling the group, Adelle was surprised that their guide was a tall, willowy young woman. Adelle's pulse quickened. She was wearing a long black cape.

The guide's name was Sofia. She explained that the sombrero represented the Spaniards who first created sherry, and the cape acknowledged students all over Portugal who traditionally wore them. Sofia, too, was a student working on an internship program with the winery.

"Welcome to our *quinta*," Sofia said, starting her presentation. "Historically, *quintas* are family-owned estates surrounded by large plots of land. I hope you enjoy your tour. We'll enjoy wine tasting afterward."

Sofia led them through the distillery in an expanded and modernized old stone building. Adelle noticed that she was staring directly at Barb when she explained that many family *quintas* in the Duoro valley had eventually sold to large corporations. Barb, however, was oblivious. As usual, she was studying her phone.

The group toured the cool, dark cellars where the grapes were pressed, made into port, then transported immediately to Porto, where the weather was better suited for storage. Next, they passed into another low-ceilinged room with large oak barrels lying on their sides, stacked in rows three high.

"I love the smell," Debbie whispered. "Time to taste the port!"

As the group walked to the wine-tasting patio overlooking the valley, Adelle turned just in time to see Barb intercepted by a man in a cape. Barb motioned for Adelle to join them.

The young man, Manuel, led Barb and Adelle into a small private tasting room lined with hundreds of dusty antique bottles stored on their sides in wooden racks.

"You are going to taste vintage port," Manuel said, directing them to a small rectangular table with a tray of glasses. He reverently selected a bottle from the rack behind the table.

"It's warehoused and shipped from Lisbon," Barb told Adelle as Manuel expertly opened the bottle.

Manuel stopped what he was doing. "That's not right," he exclaimed. "Who told you that?"

"A man I met in Porto," Barb replied.

"He doesn't know what he is talking about," Manuel said as he carefully poured out two small measures of port.

"This is a very special vintage port," he said, setting the glasses in front of Adelle and Barb. "Compliments of the family."

Adelle grinned. Being in the company of beautiful women like Barb certainly had its advantages.

"Bottoms up!" Barb said.

Manuel gasped and visibly blanched when Adelle followed Barb's lead, gulped back her port, and slammed her glass on the table. Grim-faced, he capped and packed the bottle in a small wooden box. Handing it carefully to Barb, he stopped mid-transfer and uttered a short phrase in Portuguese. Adelle asked him to write it down so she could teach the phrase to Tilly, who always said that learning a new language was good for her brain.

Adelle and Barb leaned forward together to read the phrase.

Nao partir a loica toda.

"What does that mean?" asked Barb, accepting the box from Manuel.

"Don't break the dishes," he said.

Adelle laughed to herself. Manuel had packed the bottle so well that there was no way anything was going to be broken.

"Glad you could join us for breakfast," Tilly said when Barb showed up in the ship's restaurant the next morning.

Uh-oh…

Adelle had been distracted earlier when she went to get Barb's coffee and muffin. She had started a conversation with another passenger and had stopped thinking about her only job duty. Before she knew it, breakfast was being served, and she had rushed to the restaurant, completely forgetting about Barb. The homemade bread and local jams and jellies were to die for!

"Fashion statement?" Debbie asked, pointing at Barb's rumpled sweatshirt.

"Negative," was all Barb said, motioning for Adelle to move over so she could sit facing the door.

Scooting over to another chair, Adelle felt bad. She knew Barb had spent most of the night working on the claim file.

Barb scanned the menu and glared at Adelle. "Why didn't you tell me Eggs Benedict was on the breakfast menu?"

What am I, a mind reader?

Adelle congratulated herself on using her inside voice. It was best to keep her thoughts private if she wanted to pass probation.

"Barb, are you coming to the cooking demonstration with us?" Tilly asked Barb. "The ship's chef is going to teach us how to make *Pastel de Nata*."

Adelle perked up. She loved the flaky tarts filled with delicious custard. *Pastel de Nata* was her new favorite dessert.

Ouch!

Adelle flinched when Barb kicked her under the table.

Grasping that Barb still hadn't responded to Tilly's invitation, Adelle thought quickly. Barb probably needed additional time to review more documents. Valuable time that had been wasted because she had to get her own breakfast.

"I'm going in Barb's place," Adelle said. "She's working this morning so that she can join us on the excursion this afternoon."

Adelle was relieved when Barb gave her a short nod with the hint of a smile. She had passed the mind reader test. Maybe she would pass probation after all.

"Adelle, you should pay more attention to the chef," Tilly said as the passengers stood around the demonstration table. "You could surprise Wes by baking *Pastel de Nata* for him." Adelle had already thought of surprising Wes with the delicious dessert. She had made a mental note to check with the local bakeries back home to see if they carried Portuguese pastries.

Debbie giggled. "Let me guess. You didn't get a badge for cooking either."

Adelle joined in the laughter. *Too bad there wasn't a badge for making fancy coffee or mind-reading*, she thought. Or was there? Once again, Adelle visualized the business card sample Barb had shown her at the end of their last cruise, with the phrase "and Associates."

That was the moment she had started to dream about retiring from retirement.

Suddenly, Adelle stood up straight. Instead of badges, she would earn her own business card! Barb would value her as a real Associate, not just someone acting as one for appearance's sake. Watching the chef, she wondered how she could slip the card idea into the next conversation she had with Barb.

Returning to the cabin after the morning pastry demonstration, Adelle found Barb hard at work on her laptop. She was excited to see if any progress had been made.

"Have you found out anything yet? Is the claim legit? What happens if it's not?"

"Quit asking me so many questions," Barb snapped. "I'm working on it. When I find out, I'll let you know."

Deflated, Adelle realized conversation would have to wait. Barb had been good company up until now, but Adelle knew from experience that she could get grumpy when an investigation wasn't going smoothly. She wished she could help her in some way but using technology for research definitely wasn't her strength. She would ask her about business cards later.

CHAPTER 3
CASTELO RODRIGO
EVERYTHING IN MODERATION,
INCLUDING MODERATION.

Adelle enjoyed the scenery as they sailed past more colorful hillside vineyards and cherry, almond, and olive groves. Tilly had described the view as "Mother Nature's patchwork quilt."

The drive up to Castelo Rodrigo was even more scenic, through fragrant pine forests and more almond groves. Initially, Adelle had been concerned that some of the river cruise itinerary was by motorcoach, but none of the passengers had complained. The countryside away from the river was stunning.

Adelle was relieved that Barb was sitting beside Tilly up near the front. She was still annoyed with Adelle for interrupting her work. Tilly was crocheting, and Barb was reading her phone in companionable silence.

"Did you find out what is bothering Tilly?" Debbie asked.

Adelle didn't know what to say. She wanted to be honest but didn't want to hurt Debbie's feelings.

"I'm working on it," she replied truthfully.

Castelo Rodrigo was a charming medieval village surrounded by a high stone wall. As they followed their guide through the stone gate and the steep, narrow streets, Adelle felt like she was time-traveling into the past. The site was located on a towering precipice near the Spanish border and had endured many battles over the centuries.

"These castle ruins are what gave Castelo Rodrigo its name," the guide said. Some of the old walls and doorways were still standing. With a panoramic view of the landscape below, Adelle could understand why the site had been so strategic.

"You can see for miles in all directions," Tilly said. "Just like at home."

Hearing the word 'home,' Adelle made a mental note to find out more about Tilly's farm and why she was so involved in the town nearby. Was she considering a move?

The small stone church had been founded in 1192. Inside the church, on the granite pulpit, Adelle noticed a familiar shell. The guide confirmed that the church had once been designated an important stop on the Camino de Santiago, the large network of ancient pilgrim routes stretching across Europe that converged in Santiago de Compostela in northwest Spain.

"Eventually, our village became a ghost town," the guide said. "Most of the sixteenth-century houses were abandoned. But when the government recognized Castelo Rodrigo's historical importance, it was restored. A few people have returned as permanent residents."

During free time after the walking tour, Adelle enjoyed exploring with the girls. She noticed sporadic color here and there - a planter of pink flowers, a small patch of green grass, a brightly painted red door. Given all the drab cobblestone paths and stone buildings, the touches of color brightened the mood. The feeling reminded her of the short period of dull dormant grass and leafless trees after the winter snow melted before spring started to return in all its multicolored splendor. She loved living where there were four seasons. Each had its own special quality: the migratory birds returning in the spring; golf with friends and lake time with family in the summer; the ripe bounty of fall; and the quiet wonder of winter. For Adelle, seasons represented the rhythm of life.

"Look," Debbie said, pointing. "A shop!"

Cork purses inlaid with vibrant blue cloth fluttered on a line hanging outside a stone building. Inside the shop, Adelle was amazed by all the bins of different almonds: gourmet almonds, almonds with cinnamon, salty almonds, almonds with five spices, smoked almonds, almonds with curry, and almonds with ginger. Then, Adelle spotted almonds she couldn't resist: almonds covered in chocolate.

"Almonds are good for you," Tilly said as they sampled their purchases outside while Debbie helped

Barb shop for a gift for her mother. "They lower blood sugar and cholesterol levels. And they help you sleep."

"The trick is not to eat too many," Tilly added. "They also act as a laxative." She tucked her partial bag into a pocket. "Remember, Adelle. Everything in moderation, including moderation."

Now she tells me, Adelle thought as she swallowed her last chocolate almond.

———

"Their costumes are beautiful," Debbie gushed as the girls enjoyed the evening's entertainment in the lounge. Being close to the Spanish border, three beautiful young flamenco dancers and their musicians had boarded the ship to give a performance.

"I like their tap shoes," Tilly said as she clapped along.

The music added to the party atmosphere. Barb and Adelle had shared the port Manuel had given them with Debbie and Tilly when they had arrived back on the ship, and there had been plenty of wine served at dinner that evening.

It was no surprise that when invited, most of the passengers and some crew joined the performers in a lively dance. Barb, however, stayed at the table, her thumbs tapping on her phone.

Adelle left the dance floor, hoping to persuade Barb to join the festivities.

Barb looked up at her and pursed her lips before

speaking. Over the music, clapping, and laughter, all Adelle could hear was, "…failed the test."

Adelle was devastated. She had failed probation. "Does that mean I won't get a business card?" she blurted out as she dropped into the chair beside Barb.

Barb stared at her. "The port failed the test," she finally said. "It was not the port the buyer ordered. So the claim is legit."

When Adelle made the mistake of asking her about the test, Barb leaned forward and launched into a detailed lecture about using Carbon 14 analysis.

"What happens now?" Adelle interjected the moment Barb paused for breath.

"I've let the intern know the findings. Now we can start the recovery phase."

Adelle briefly debated if she should ask what the recovery phase entailed, but when the band started playing another lively song, she impulsively jumped up and reached out for Barb's hand. "That can wait. It's time to dance with Debbie and Tilly!"

As Adelle left the lounge at the end of the evening, Amelia asked her what she had enjoyed the most on the trip so far. Adelle couldn't choose one experience over another. It had all been so rejuvenating.

"I noticed you had your own private tasting at the port winery," Amelia said. "That hasn't happened before."

Adelle described the room and the port in the dusty bottle.

"Vintage port!" Amelia exclaimed, clapping her

hands together. "You were very fortunate. Some of it is very expensive."

"It must be," Adelle said, describing how carefully Manuel had packaged the remaining port for Barb. "Maybe that's why he told us not to *partir a loica toda*. Not to break the dishes."

Amelia raised her eyebrow. "In Portuguese, to break the dishes is to cause problems. Perhaps he was warning you not to cause problems."

Adelle chuckled. What problems could they possibly cause?

CHAPTER 4
SALAMANCA
WHERE IS WALDO?

Most of the passengers, including Adelle, napped on the long motorcoach drive to Salamanca the next morning. She had been up later than normal the night before, thanks to her friend back home, who had taught Adelle to alternate each glass of wine with a glass of water. The almonds hadn't helped.

Salamanca was stunning. Refreshed after the motor-coach trip, Adelle was enjoying the walking tour with the local guide. The first stop was the central market. As they strolled under the high roof, the brightly colored veggies, fruit, and various smells reminded Adelle of her first experience in a European market in Budapest. She enjoyed sampling a variety of Iberian hams, fresh cheese, olives, and wine.

"It's five o'clock somewhere," Debbie said, raising her glass in a toast.

From the market, they proceeded to Plaza Mayor,

"the heart of Salamanca," according to their guide. The large public square was built in the Baroque style between 1729 and 1755 and had been used for bull-fighting up until the nineteenth century. Passing through the arched gate in the wall, they were surrounded by golden sandstone walls, four stories high.

"Look at the storks on that bell tower," Debbie said, digging her phone out of her purse to take a picture. "They have the best view."

Their guide pointed to a building with five granite arches. "That is the old City Hall," he began. Adelle missed what he said next. She was captivated by another glowing sandstone wall featuring balconies over the shops in the semicircular arches below.

"There are 247 balconies," the guide told them. "They belong to private residents."

Adelle chuckled when Tilly asked him to repeat the number of balconies. Amelia had told them there would be a trivia contest on the last night of their river cruise. Tilly was determined to win. *Who knows*, thought Adelle. Perhaps 247 would be the winning answer.

The guide took them to the center of the square. "This plaque commemorates the declaration of the old city of Salamanca as a UNESCO World Heritage site."

"Another picture to send to Teresa," Debbie said, taking a photo before they continued their walking tour near the square.

"Look at that building," Debbie exclaimed, gesturing at the walls covered with hundreds of carvings of scallop shells.

"That house was built between 1493 and 1517," their guide said. "It was the residence of the knight of the Order of Santiago, Don Rodrigo Garcia Maldonado. In addition to the shells, notice the many coats of arms around the windows and doorways. Today the building houses an art gallery and the Salamanca public library." It was the most interesting library building Adelle had ever seen.

The next destination was Salamanca University, founded in 1134 and considered one of the world's finest. It was the oldest university in Spain and all of Europe. Looking up at the famous façade of the Escuelas Mayores building, Adelle was hard-pressed to identify the various historical figures embedded in the carvings.

"This beautiful work of art is from the sixteenth century," the guide said. "See if you can find the famous frog."

"This reminds me of playing 'Where's Waldo' with my grandkids," Tilly said. She wouldn't leave until she found it.

Nearby was the Old Cathedral, which dated back to the twelfth century, and the New Cathedral, built from 1513 through 1733.

"I love traveling in Europe," Debbie gushed. "If three hundred years ago is *new*, we must be youngsters!"

"There are many mysterious carvings in Salamanca," the guide said, pointing to the detailed façade of the New Cathedral. "See if you can find some of them on this wall."

Some of the passengers from their group started to chuckle. Adelle looked where they were looking. Beside the cathedral's lateral door, amongst the usual gothic monsters and gargoyles, Adelle was surprised to see what was clearly an astronaut.

That's impossible. There were definitely no astronauts back in the seventeenth century.

Near the astronaut, Adelle picked out a mischievous little gargoyle, smirking as he ate an ice cream cone. Another impossibility.

Adelle was amused when the guide explained the mystery. The carvings were both added in 1992 by stonemasons doing some restoration work on the cathedral.

"Leaving their legacy cast in stone," Debbie quipped.

As they were given time to explore on their own, Adelle spotted green trees and shrubs through a small archway built into a stone wall at the end of a narrow cobblestone street. She led the girls into the hidden park, an oasis of color on the edge of the city center. While Adelle and Debbie walked and chatted and shared stories about their university days, Adelle noticed Barb and Tilly sitting on a stone bench, engaged in a very serious conversation. Adelle wondered if Barb knew anything about community fundraising. Somehow, she doubted it.

Climbing a narrow stairway to an upstairs restaurant for a tapas lunch, Adelle was surprised at how hungry she was. All the fresh air and intellectual stimulation had also stimulated her appetite. She laughed as she caught herself thinking that perhaps Barb was right. It was time to refuel.

The creamy *pincho de tortilla* was delicious. It was a cross between scrambled eggs and a potato pie without the crust, sliced into portions and served on a piece of baguette.

Adelle's next choice was *queso de cabra con arandonos*, goat cheese with cranberries, followed by a *montadito*, a small sandwich filled with cured ham, pork tenderloin, and cheese.

"Don't eat too much, Adelle," Debbie said. "You'll be too full to go shopping with us."

"Too late," Adelle replied, grinning as she sat back and patted her stomach.

Adelle was content to sit by herself at the outside cafe as the sisters shopped for souvenirs, and Barb ran an errand. Earlier, while eating lunch and looking out the window overlooking the plaza, she had noticed a well-dressed man sitting alone at a café table piled with packages. When a woman added another parcel before hurrying away, Adelle had a bright idea. She could volunteer to sit in the central location and watch over parcels.

Dunking churros into her chocolate sauce, Adelle was reminded of her grandson. No matter how much he ate, he always had room for dessert. He claimed it was for a different part of his stomach. Adelle reflected on what she knew about the investigation so far. Barb had explained that there were millionaires who collected rare wine like ordinary people collected coins or stamps. A wine distributor bought a rare port on behalf of a valued customer, but what they ordered wasn't what had been received. The distributor had submitted a seven-figure claim. Now that the claim appeared legitimate, the investigation had entered the recovery phase.

"The insurance company is entitled to recover the cost of the claim," Barb had explained earlier that morning. "When we get back to Porto, I'm going to try and find the missing port." Adelle hoped she was off probation by then. She wanted to help in the search.

Adelle jumped and dropped her churro on the ground as packages rained down on her table.

"The Italians are drug pushers," Tilly said, scowling as she sat down.

"What Italians?" Adelle asked, longing to pick up the churro. Did the five-second rule apply in Portugal?

Leave it there, Adelle.

"The loud, obnoxious group from our ship."

Tilly had complained before about the boisterous family disturbing her quiet time on the deck. Adelle had spoken briefly to a woman from their group the first morning they were on the ship. She was standing behind her in the omelet line. "Standing in lineups is the only quiet time I ever get," the woman had commented when Adelle attempted to chit chat. Adelle took the hint. Later, she understood where the woman was coming from. The family stuck together on every excursion. Adelle hadn't had the opportunity to talk to her again.

"I overheard them talking," Tilly said, crossing her arms.

Adelle wasn't surprised. Tilly was always eavesdropping. She called it *rubbernecking*.

More parcels showered onto the table.

"I need some help here," Debbie said, struggling to hold onto many small bags and a small cardboard box.

As Adelle jumped up to help her with her parcels, Debbie chatted animatedly about each purchase, where she bought them, and who they were for. She opened one of the boxes to show Adelle eight small chocolate cupcakes decorated with tiny orange and white flowers. Adelle assumed they were to share with port at "yappy hour" later on the ship's deck. Drooling over the prospect of more chocolate, Adelle knew she couldn't wait that long for one of her cupcakes.

Looking across the square, Adelle was surprised to see Barb in conversation with a dark-haired man. When Barb looked their way, Adelle waved to catch her attention and let her know where they were seated. Suddenly, she had a perfect idea.

"Here comes Barb," Adelle said. "What a great photo opportunity!"

When the sisters turned toward Barb, Adelle snatched one of the cupcakes, dunked it in her chocolate sauce, and took a bite.

What?

She swore, grabbed her napkin, and spit it out.

Tilly spun around. "Someone with a potty mouth needs to wash her mouth out with soap."

Debbie burst out laughing. "I think she just did."

Sure enough, the cupcakes were decorated soaps.

After joining in the laughter, Adelle kept apologizing.

"It makes no never mind," Debbie and Tilly said together.

"It makes no never mind," Adelle repeated. She had forgotten that expression. On a previous trip, the sisters had talked about growing up with other families who had settled in their area. Some of the local sayings were hilarious.

"Don't worry about it, Adelle." Debbie's eyes were twinkling. "Now we have an excuse to go back to that cute soap shop."

Barb offered to help Adelle carry the parcels and meet the sisters at the motorcoach at 3:00. In return, they agreed to purchase soap cupcakes for Barb's mother.

"Don't buy any port from strangers on the street," Barb warned them before they left.

"What was that all about?" Adelle asked Barb as they watched the sisters head across the square.

"Remember John, the man I met at the Port House in Porto?" Barb asked.

The dark-haired man, Adelle realized, nodding. In her excitement about the cupcakes, she had forgotten all about him.

"I just ran into him, and that's what he told me."

Barb frowned. "Disreputable people are probably scamming tourists by passing off cheap bottles of port as the more expensive varieties."

"Speaking of passing," Adelle blurted, "am I still on probation?" The concept was really starting to annoy her. She wasn't fresh out of university working on her first job; she was in her sixties, for goodness sake!

Barb smirked as she handed her a palm-sized cardboard box. "I had these made for you."

Adelle opened the box. They were business cards! With her name on them! She squinted to read the small print under her name:

Junior associate.

Junior?

Adelle closed her eyes. She had two choices. She could try and explain how insulted she was and give them back, or she could accept them gratefully. If she gave them back, that would be the end of retiring from retirement. She would once again be facing a boring future. But if she accepted the cards, she would also have to accept her "junior" status.

At least you're off probation, Adelle.

"Thank you," she said.

"You're welcome." Barb frowned. "I tried to call you from the fast print shop to see if you wanted a middle initial included, but your phone is turned off."

Adelle admitted to Barb that she didn't have an international package. She didn't need the camera option; Debbie shared her photos after each trip. She didn't need an alarm; she knew Barb would wake her up each morning. Getting a phone package hadn't made any sense. All Adelle used her phone for was the odd free text here and there with friends and family back home. The only reason she had brought it to Salamanca in the first place was to please Barb. To avoid any costly roaming charges, she had simply turned her phone off.

Barb sighed. "You can use your phone camera and alarm without a package." She went on to list other free functions, but Adelle stopped listening after she looked down. All she could see and hear was her half-eaten churro, lying on the ground, calling her name.

Barb coughed. "We need to be able to call each other." She explained how she could set Adelle's phone up to make and receive international calls, but Adelle was focused on a different objective.

"I'll be right back," Adelle said, jumping up. "Do you want a churro with chocolate sauce?"

"No," Barb replied, letting out a sigh. "I'll wait here until you get back." She picked up her phone. "The intern suggested the print shop. I'll text him to refer me to a reliable mobile store near here."

Adelle enjoyed her second churro as she sat in the warm afternoon sunshine, daydreaming and watching people. River cruising was so relaxing - she was learning about different cultures, wining and dining, and having fun with her girlfriends. A shadow fell across the parcels on the table. Adelle looked up to see a stork flying towards its nest above the clock on the bell tower. She was shocked to see that it was already 2:45. Barb had promised to be back by 2:45, but she was nowhere to be seen. Adelle started to fidget. That wasn't like Barb. She was always punctual to the minute.

Adelle began to worry. How would she carry all the packages back to the motorcoach by herself?

At 2:50, Adelle wondered what would happen if they missed the motor coach drive back to the ship.

At 3:00, Adelle started to panic. If she shoved everything in the biggest bag and walked really fast, she could probably get to the motorcoach on time and persuade Amelia to wait for Barb. She berated herself for not being able to use her phone to call Debbie, Tilly, or Barb.

The sisters will stall for you, Adelle. Wait for Barb.

Searching the square, she saw a group of students wearing capes. They reminded Adelle of Manuel at the port winery. Why had he given Barb and her a private tasting? Why had he given them an expensive vintage port?

Adelle's stomach clenched. Was it a bottle of rare port like the port that was missing? She tried to recall what Manuel had said as he had carefully handed Barb the dusty bottle. Her heart started to race. "Compliments of the family," he had said, looking cross.

Family. Tilly had just mentioned the Italian family onboard their ship. They were drug pushers, she had said. Were they part of the Mafia family? And what about Manuel? He had warned them not to cause problems. Was he involved, too? What else had he said? She remembered how upset he was when Barb told him that vintage port was shipped to Lisbon. Why had John misled Barb? Adelle's spider senses went into over-drive. John was in Salamanca. Was there a connection?

Adelle anxiously searched the square again for Barb, remembering what she had said earlier. Desperate people do desperate things. With millions of dollars of port involved, there was a lot at stake. Barb must be in danger; otherwise, she would be on time. Maybe she had been abducted by the mob!

Breathe, Adelle, breathe.

Adelle shrieked when Barb plopped down on the chair beside her.

"Where have you been?" Adelle demanded. "It's 3:45. You're an hour late!"

"Don't be such a drama queen," Barb replied. "It's only 2:45."

Drama queen? The nerve!

Adelle pointed at the clock across the square.

Barb smirked. "Obviously, you weren't paying attention when Amelia told us about the time change between Spain and Portugal."

Uh-oh ...

Adelle clutched her hands in her lap, trying to stop them from trembling. She had put one and one together and had come up with three.

Relax, Adelle. Barb is okay.

Adelle rolled her shoulders and stretched her neck.

She'll probably put you on probation again.

Adelle really didn't want that. Junior Associate was bad enough.

Think, Adelle.

She smiled when she realized she could steal a page out of Barb's book.

"I was just testing," Adelle said, faking a laugh. "You passed."

CHAPTER 5
FAVAIOS
GO COMB MONKEYS

The next morning, on the walking tour through the small village of Favaios, Adelle could smell the first destination before they arrived. There was nothing like the aroma of freshly baked bread. It reminded her of visiting her grandparents on their farm when she was little. Air buns, smothered in butter and honey straight from the hive, were her favorite.

The owner and chief baker, dressed in her white baker's hat and apron, welcomed them to her traditional bakery, where the bread was baked in an oven heated with wood and old grapevines. Their handsome young guide explained that bread in the family bakery had been made the same way for centuries. The oven was modeled after those left behind by the Roman occupation. Once again, Adelle was struck by the Roman's influence, even as far away as Portugal.

The baker had burned pine branches for several hours that morning to get the heat where she liked it.

The guide assisted the baker as she put one loaf at a time on a wooden paddle and pushed it into the depths of the oven. While they were baking, she started work on the next batch. "She makes around 500 loaves per day," their guide explained. Working on a square table dusted with flour, the baker expertly cut the dough and then twisted the pieces in half. As she set the loaves aside to rise for half an hour, a phone pinged.

Adelle checked her phone. After their day in Sala-manca, Barb had set it up for international calls and insisted that Adelle carry it at all times. She breathed a sigh of relief. She had remembered to put it on silent mode before they entered the building.

The baker frowned and shook her head as Barb studied her phone and then gestured to Tilly to follow her outside. Adelle was sure she heard the baker mutter "*nao partir a loica toda*," before she turned to take fresh loaves out of the oven.

"More samples for us," Debbie said, watching her sister leave. Adelle agreed as she slathered butter on the freshly baked bread. Crackly on the outside but light and moist inside, the butter melted into the fluffy center. Adelle closed her eyes and sighed as she took her first bite. She was in her happy place.

The next stop on their walking tour was the Favaios Bread and Wine Museum, housed in a building dating from the eighteenth century and dedicated to the local bread and Muscatel wine. Their museum host was a passionate young woman who strolled with them through the exhibitions. There was an interactive station where participants could play simple computer games to understand the bread-making process. Adelle preferred the station where she could test her sense of smell by inhaling the various aromas associated with Muscatel wine. She also enjoyed the display that showed how the color of Muscatel wine changed from a pale salmon color to a dark caramel as it aged. Afterward, when they sampled the wine on the museum terrace, Adelle was able to articulate how the younger wine was light, fresh, floral, and fruity compared to the rich toffee taste of the ten-year version.

Adelle saw Barb and Tilly huddling in the corner of the terrace. As she wondered what they were up to, an unpleasant thought surfaced. Tilly was older and wiser than Adelle. And she certainly wasn't a drama queen. Did Adelle have competition for the coveted Associate position?

Adelle shook her head. They were probably talking about fundraising. But why would Tilly talk to Barb about fundraising? Adelle was sure she knew more about fundraising than Barb did. Didn't she?

You haven't come up with any ideas for Tilly yet.

Adelle knew she needed more information to stoke the *idea* fires, including finding out more about Tilly's town. She decided to ride with her on the motorcoach to their next destination and practice her interrogation skills.

"The name of the town near our farm is Orcadia, named by my great grandfather," Tilly said with pride. He had been one of the first settlers in the area, she continued. "He emigrated from Scotland. In 1882, only twenty years old, he left his widowed mother and three brothers on their farm in one of Orkney's north islands to homestead in Canada. First, he took a small boat used to transport passengers, mail, and freight amongst the small islands to Kirkwall. 'Orcadia' was the name of the boat."

Tilly was very proud of her heritage. Her great grandfather had traveled to Glasgow from Kirkwall, where he booked his passage to a new life. After sailing across the ocean and up the Gulf of St. Lawrence to Quebec, he had taken the train westward to Winnipeg.

"He walked the last one hundred miles," Tilly said. "After staking his claim, his mother, brothers, and other families from the Orkneys joined him the following year."

Tilly obviously loved living on the family farm. "We still farm the land our great grandfather homesteaded," she proudly said.

Adelle was curious how she had become so involved in the nearby town of Orcadia. "It can be a long winter living in the country," Tilly replied. "I have lots of friends in town."

"Do you think you will move there someday?"

Tilly frowned. "My husband is talking about passing our farmhouse on to our grandson," she replied. "But I'm not ready for that yet." Pulling out her crocheting, Tilly signaled that their conversation was over.

Arriving at a historic *quinta* for lunch, the motorcoach was greeted by three men singing and playing musical instruments. Adelle soon learned that the accordion player was also the proprietor of the estate. He was very expressive, like a child in a grown man's body. His eyes opened wide as he spoke, and his hands flew, almost as much as Debbie's hands when she was excited. He reminded Adelle of someone she knew. Who?

"He is the Portuguese Mr. Bean," Amelia replied, grinning.

Of course!

"Who is Mr. Bean?" Barb asked.

"Have you never watched Mr. Bean?" Tilly asked incredulously. "He was on a famous British sitcom in the early nineties."

Barb smirked. "I was a baby in the early nineties."

"Then you don't know what you were missing," Tilly said, rolling her eyes.

As they followed the proprietor through the wine cellar, Adelle was astounded by the size of the barrels containing the *quinta's* Muscatel wine.

"The Muscatel that we have in the first 30,000-liter barrel, almost 9,000 gallons for some of you, is Muscatel from my family," he said proudly. "It is fifty years old. In the second and third barrels, we keep the Muscatel from my grandfather. It is seventy years old. In barrels four and five…," he paused, scanned his audience, opened his eyes even wider, and shrugged. "In barrels, four and five," he repeated, "we keep … nothing!" He mimicked drinking wine as he laughed. "We already drank it!"

Adelle laughed with the others. He was very entertaining.

"Seriously though, barrels four and five contain wine from my great grandfather. It is 120 years old." The proprietor shrugged. "It is what we do. We make Muscatel, and we keep some for the next generation."

Another family legacy.

Adelle enjoyed the delicious lunch served on the *quinta's* patio overlooking the valley below. They started with a special hearty soup.

"The soup is named after a local woman, Antonia," the proprietor told them. "About one hundred years ago, when there was a grape disease, she saved local farmers with her nutritious soup. Otherwise, their families would have gone hungry and had to sell their properties at depressed prices. But thanks to Antonia, they didn't quit." He raised his glass. "To Antonia."

The next course was a mouthwatering veal loaf stewed in red wine. Following that, Adelle chose the "drunken pears" for dessert. The pears had been marinated in red wine and sugar and were to die for. She wondered if their group had enjoyed too much wine when Tilly approached the proprietor, and he handed her his accordion.

"Sis, I didn't know you played the accordion," Debbie said when Tilly returned to their table after curtsying to rousing applause.

"You don't know everything about me," Tilly replied, winking at Barb.

What was that all about? Adelle wondered. She had seen Tilly and Barb talking earnestly again as they tasted wine on the patio overlooking the hillside. Something was definitely up.

On the ride back to the ship, Amelia sat down beside Adelle. She shared that after large corporations had taken over many small, family-run *quintas*, the area had been revived thanks to tourism. River cruises on the Duoro had helped spur social and economic development in the region. Amelia said that about half of the thousand residents of Favaios were involved in one way or another with the village wine cooperative.

"Did you notice that our servers at lunch were the young man who took us to the bakery and the young woman who conducted the tour of the museum?" Amelia asked.

Now that Amelia mentioned it, Adelle felt foolish. Barb was right. She needed to be more observant.

As Adelle settled in for a short nap before the motorcoach arrived back at the ship, she reflected on their excursions that day. She was inspired by the example of the Favaios cooperative and the generations coming together to preserve their tradition and way of life. Drifting off, she thought of the town of Orcadia. An idea was starting to germinate.

After dinner on board that night, the passengers were entertained by a Tuna Folk Band. Amelia explained that tuna folk bands had been customary since the thirteenth century. They were made up of university students in traditional dress, singing serenades and playing traditional instruments to earn spending money. Between sets, Adelle chuckled when Tilly asked Debbie to take her picture with the young men dressed in their black suits, vests, and ties.

"I thought Tilly hates having her picture taken," Barb said, smirking.

"Not when handsome young men are involved," Adelle replied. "It runs in the family," she said, pointing at Debbie, who was taking her turn posing with the band.

"Looks like it's time for another 'girls' photo," Barb said, standing up as Debbie waved.

Heading back to their table, Adelle was startled when her phone rang. She hurried out to the deck, where it was quieter.

"Hello," she answered on the fourth ring.

Adelle was shocked by the torrent of Portuguese. Adelle couldn't understand what the obviously angry woman said other than "*familia*" and "*sposa*." At the end of the short call, Adelle was sure she heard "go comb monkeys."

Puzzled, Adelle went back to the lounge to find Amelia. She spotted her talking to Tilly and Barb.

"We have a research question for you," Adelle heard Tilly ask Amelia as she approached them. Adelle stopped in her tracks. Her intuition had been right. Tilly was working with Barb now. She was tempted to leave, but wanted to know what they were researching.

Adelle, Tilly likes learning foreign phrases.

"I have a question, too," Adelle said as she joined them. "What does 'go comb monkeys' mean?"

"Get lost or drop dead," Amelia replied.

Lying in bed that night, Adelle considered her choices. She could keep the angry phone call to herself and spend the rest of the trip worrying about it, or she could tell Barb, who would probably accuse her of being a drama queen again. Or worse, being a rookie. She needed to do more research before she said anything.

Reminded of research, she wondered what Tilly and Barb were going to ask Amelia earlier. She had been so shocked by the "drop dead" translation that she had returned to her cabin before hearing their question.

Was it really possible that Tilly was competing for the Associate position? After all, Tilly was very competitive about everything. She reminded Adelle of her grandson. When she told him she tried to drink six glasses of water a day, he insisted on drinking seven. His attitude was evident in sports, where he excelled at hockey and basketball.

Adelle was okay with competition to a point. Win the things that count, she reminded herself. She really wanted the Associate position.

You haven't done anything other than make coffee.

True, but she wished Barb would give her another duty. What was holding her back?

What about danger?

Was Barb shielding her from danger? Maybe the call was legit, like the claim.

Was it a warning?

Adelle shivered. After turning the heat up in their cabin, being careful not to wake Barb, she crept back to bed. She knew she had a lot to learn about being an investigator. Barb had tried to tell her, but it hadn't taken hold. *Yet.*

Burrowing under the blankets, Adelle tried to recall Barb's lessons.

Be observant.

She replayed the call in her mind. The caller was female, she was angry, and she had threatened Adelle. Or had she? Perhaps the caller had the wrong number. She sighed with relief. Yes, that had to be it.

What about "sposa?"

Adelle's eyes flew open again. Were the Italians members of the Sposa family? That sounded like a mob name! She shivered again as she replayed what the angry caller had said. She wanted Adelle to drop dead.

Pulling the covers up tight under her chin, she was tempted to give her business cards back to Barb and quit. Tilly could have the Associate job.

What if Barb and Tilly are in danger?

Thinking of Antonia, who had saved her friends and

neighbors with her hearty soup, Adelle knew she couldn't quit.

You can do it, Adelle. Be brave. Be diligent.

Adelle gave up trying to get some sleep. She needed a plan.

CHAPTER 6
LAMEGO

EVERYONE SHOULD DO WHAT THEY DO BEST

"This is the Sanctuary of Our Lady of Remedies," their guide said as they disembarked from the motorcoach at the top of the hill overlooking the small town of Lamego. Adelle's stomach rumbled. She didn't know if it was from a lack of sleep, picking nervously at breakfast, or fear. Regardless, it was time to put her plan into action.

Adelle saw the Italians huddled together in front of the Sanctuary. She took a deep breath and walked toward them. As she approached the family, she heard conversations sprinkled with Italian, French, and English. The woman she had met in line at the ship was talking loudly to an elderly man. As they turned toward her, he pointed and spoke rapidly. Adelle didn't know much Italian or French. But she knew "shoot." She froze.

There was nowhere to hide. Adelle threw her hands in the air in surrender as the woman walked towards her, arm extended. Adelle closed her eyes and braced for impact.

"My papa would like you to shoot our picture," the woman said, holding out her phone.

Adelle laughed at herself as she suddenly recalled Barb's lesson to not assume. Chatting with the woman, she discovered that the family were Canadians from Montreal.

"The Lady of Remedies is very important to our family," Adelle's new friend told her later as they stood at the top of the grand double staircase.

"Are you pilgrims?" Adelle asked. The guide had told them how the devout climbed the 686 steps of the staircase up to the eighteenth-century baroque chapel, sometimes on their knees.

The woman chuckled. "Sorry to disappoint you. We're three generations of pharmacists."

"Drug pushers," Adelle blurted. She covered her mouth with her hand. She couldn't believe she had just said that.

Fortunately, her new friend had a good sense of humor. It wasn't the first time she had been called a drug pusher.

After taking a few more photos of the family, Adelle started to walk down the staircase. There were nine terraces, each decorated with *azulejo* tiles and decorative urns. Watching each step carefully so she didn't trip, she reached the fourth terrace. Looking up, she saw Barb standing by the railing, hunched over with her hands on her knees.

"Are you okay?" Adelle asked, rushing toward her.

Barb nodded. Her face was flushed, and she was breathing rapidly. She held up her hand. "Catching my breath," she managed to say.

After Barb recovered, she told Adelle that she had decided to test her fitness level by running up the staircase. She was more than happy to quit at the halfway point and walk back down with Adelle.

"I met Tilly's Italian drug pushers," Adelle blurted out.

"You mean the pharmacist family from Montreal?" Barb asked.

Adelle stopped walking. "Does Tilly know that about them?"

"She's the one who told me."

Adelle digested the news. Something didn't make sense.

"Why is she so against them?" Adelle asked. It couldn't be because they were so boisterous. Her own sister was easily as loud and outgoing.

"I can't say."

For goodness sake. Barb could be so frustrating. Adelle tried another question. She had nothing to lose. "What is Tilly researching today?"

"She's looking for blue and white yarn." Barb pointed up at the tile scene behind them. "We want to crochet a blanket in these colors as a gift for my mother."

Adelle felt foolish. She had made another wrong

assumption. Or had she? That still didn't explain all the other whispered conversations.

Be brave, Adelle. "We're partners, right?"

"Affirmative," Barb replied.

Adelle took a deep breath. "Then I need to know what you know. What have you and Tilly been talking about?"

Barb sighed. "I will tell you, but it has to remain confidential."

"Affirmative," Adelle replied.

Barb explained that Tilly had been the victim of an internet scam.

"It's partially my fault," she said. "Seniors are the most frequent targets. I taught her how to Google on the internet, but I didn't teach her how to watch out for scams."

Tilly had discovered a company that offered anti-aging supplements guaranteed to help people live longer. Intrigued, she had emailed them for the free trial offer.

"Did she give them her credit card number?" Adelle asked.

"No. When they asked for it, she refused. Since the trial was free, she reasoned that they didn't need her credit card number."

"What did she do then?"

"She stopped using technology."

So that's why she chose not to bring her phone, Adelle realized.

"Have you been able to help her?"

"Affirmative. I've contacted the authorities about the scam. It's been shut down."

Adelle was relieved. Justice had been served.

Continuing to make their way down the staircase, Adelle was thankful she hadn't mentioned her fears about Tilly competing for her job. Secure in her position again, she put her investigator's hat back on. "Where are we meeting the intern tonight?" she asked.

"At the Port House in Porto."

Adelle regretted that, thanks to her, Barb had missed her meeting. "The same Port House as your original meeting?"

"Affirmative. Same place. Same time." Barb looked serious. "We need to find the missing port. My new career depends on it."

Adelle agreed. So did hers.

Sitting on the ship's deck after lunch, Tilly asked Adelle to give crocheting another try. Adelle was still feeling bad about thinking poorly of her older friend earlier, so she agreed. As she struggled to tie the first knot, she understood why Tilly had not told her family that she had been scammed. She was embarrassed.

"Sorry, I'm not good at crocheting," Adelle said, blushing, as she handed the hook and yarn back to Tilly.

"It makes no never mind," Tilly said. "Everyone should do what they do best." In a flash, she tied a knot and started a new square. "Have you come up with any fundraising ideas?"

Before revealing what she was contemplating, Adelle saw Debbie walking toward them. She smiled, remembering the conversation she had enjoyed with Debbie at the coffee station that morning.

"Adelle, I didn't get a chance yet to show you the Portuguese roosters I've been buying for some of my customers," Debbie had said, eyes twinkling. She had reached into her new cork purse and pulled out a brightly painted rooster the size of her palm. "It's called a *Barcelos* rooster. The rooster is a Portuguese symbol of faith, good luck, and justice. I plan on giving them to my less fortunate customers by sneaking them into their parcels."

Debbie was one of the most kind-hearted, generous women Adelle had ever met. It bothered her that Tilly wouldn't tell her about her fundraising problem.

Everyone deserves a second chance.

Deciding on the spot that Debbie needed to be Tilly's fundraising hero, Adelle smiled. "I'm working on it," she replied.

CHAPTER 7
PORTO
A SECOND CHANCE

As Adelle and Barb walked to the Port House that night, Barb suddenly stopped and slapped her thigh. "I left my cellphone charging in our cabin." She spun around. "Go ahead, I'll catch up with you," she called over her shoulder as she sprinted back to the ship.

"Make sure the sisters don't nab you for the trivia contest," Adelle shouted.

Barb raised her hand in acknowledgment.

Continuing toward the Port House, Adelle chuckled to herself. Earlier at dinner, Barb had announced that the two of them had a meeting and would miss the one and only trivia contest of the trip.

When Debbie had asked about the meeting, Tilly reminded her that Barb's work was confidential and deftly changed the topic. On the one hand, Adelle was slightly hurt that neither of the sisters had questioned why she was involved. But, on the other hand, she was thankful she didn't have to divulge her Junior Associate status.

The night was clear and beautiful. Was it only a week ago that she had been trembling, shrouded in fog and darkness as Amelia accompanied her to find Barb? It seemed like a lifetime ago. Adelle admired the *rabelos* bobbing in the water next to the boardwalk, framed by the lights of Porto twinkling across the Duoro. Although she wanted to stop and enjoy the sights, there was work to do. She strode confidently through the door of the Port House.

Adelle chose the table in the back corner, confident that Barb would find her there. She left the seat facing the door vacant for Barb and sat with her back to the band.

Adelle noticed a dark-haired man slipping through a door in the back wall. She was sure it was John, the man Barb had been talking to in Salamanca. The same man who had introduced himself to Barb a week ago. Was it just a coincidence? Adelle didn't think so. Looking over her shoulder, there was still no sign of Barb. Then, as her spider senses started to tingle, she made a quick decision.

The door clicked shut behind her as Adelle followed John into the dark room. As her eyes adjusted, she could barely make out the rows of barrels stacked on top of each other on either side of the wide aisle. She deduced that she was in a warehouse.

Guided by a faint light at the far end of the large room, Adelle tiptoed forward. The light was coming from her left. She carefully peeked around the corner. John was attaching a padlock to a cabinet with bars across the doors. Was that a gun in his other hand?

Click!

Whirling around, Adelle saw a slim beam of light just before the entrance door closed again. Someone else had followed them. She ducked behind the barrels to her right. Across the aisle, she saw a shadow creep stealthily between the barrels and the far wall. Adelle caught her breath. He was carrying a rifle!

Panicking, Adelle turned to run back to the entrance, but she tripped in her haste and fell down on her bruised knee. Her potty mouth gave her away.

Scrambling to get up, Adelle was blinded by a bright light. Images of her family flashed through her mind. Would she see her youngest granddaughter grow up, get married, and start a family of her own? She knew her mind, just like the rest of Adelle's grandchildren. Adelle visualized her granddaughter as a young toddler, barely old enough to sit in her high chair by herself. Whenever she was finished eating, she would yell "done!" and sweep everything off her tray onto the floor.

Adelle realized that she was done, too. She was done with being afraid of her own shadow, done with worrying all the time, done with cowering.

"Turn that light off," Adelle demanded as she stood up.

The room was once again plunged into darkness.

"Are you okay?" a male voice asked.

Before she could respond, the entrance door opened

briefly, let in a flash of light, and closed again. Then, she heard an angry Portuguese woman. Adelle would never forget that voice. It was the threatening caller.

Suddenly, the overhead lights came on. Adelle recognized the woman at the light switch by the door. She was the very pregnant woman Adelle had briefly met at the Port House the previous week. Adelle turned around to face her assailants, then sighed with relief. John wasn't carrying a gun; he was cradling a bottle of wine under his arm. The man beside him wasn't holding a rifle; he was carrying a mandolin. Her relief was short-lived.

Adelle was caught in the middle of rapid-fire Portuguese as the man and woman turned on John and scolded him. The woman jabbed him in the chest. The man repeatedly thrust his mandolin at John, emphatically punctuating each outburst. Feeling sorry for John, Adelle faked a loud cough to make her presence known. The room went silent as the trio turned and stared at her.

"Who are you?" John challenged. "You are trespassing."

Adelle had learned her lesson. Honesty was the best policy. She handed him her business card. "I'm investigating a case," she said, with as much authority as she could muster under the circumstances.

The woman grabbed the card and read it. She kept looking back and forth between the card and Adelle. "You are "Junior"? she asked in halting English.

Adelle bristled with indignation.

You need a promotion, Adelle.

She nodded.

The trio burst out laughing. After another conversation that Adelle couldn't understand, other than "*sposa*" and "*familia*," the woman threw her arms around John and hugged him.

It was Adelle's turn to demand some answers. "What is going on?"

The couple deferred to the younger man.

"John is my big brother, and she is his wife," the young man said after introducing himself as Barb's contact, the intern. His eyes sparkled. "They are expecting their first child. A boy."

Adelle relaxed. Nothing made her feel better than the miracle of babies, except perhaps chocolate. After congratulating the young couple, Adelle suggested John take his wife back to sit down and take the weight off her feet. "If you see Barb, could you bring her back here, please?"

John nodded as he carefully passed the bottle from under his arm to his brother before escorting his wife back down the aisle.

"Follow me," the intern said. He led Adelle back to the locked cabinet where she had found John earlier. She could see dusty bottles in racks behind the barred glass doors.

"Hold this, please." The intern passed his mandolin to Adelle, knelt down, unlocked the cabinet, and reverently returned the dusty bottle to the rack. Noticing the empty space beside it, Adelle bent over to take a closer look. The labels matched the bottle that Manuel had presented to Barb.

"This is a rare port my grandfather's family produced," the intern said proudly.

"Why is it here?" Adelle asked.

"My grandfather sold the family *quinta* to a corporation with the stipulation that they manage the remaining vintage port. He wanted to be sure that future generations would be taken care of."

Adelle thought of Amelia and her grandfather, Mr. Bean and his family, and all the local stories she had heard on her river cruise. Family was important in Portugal.

"My brother works here, operating the forklift." He shrugged. "He is fortunate to have this job. He did poorly in school."

Everyone should do what they do best, Adelle thought.

"The company is paying my way through university," the intern continued, dusting his hands off on his black pants. "They have promised me a manager-trainee position with them when I graduate."

As Adelle handed the mandolin back, she heard the familiar click of the closing entrance door. John and Barb joined them shortly afterward.

After introductions, Barb glared at the intern and got right to the point. "We are here to recover the missing port. You texted you had important information to share."

The intern explained what had happened to the

missing port while his brother stood shame-faced beside him. Distracted by thoughts of fatherhood, John had made an error. He had loaded the wrong port to be shipped to the distributor.

"Was it supposed to be this port?" Adelle asked, pointing to the cabinet. Was it an innocent mistake, or had John prevented the family treasure from being sold, thus keeping it for the next generation?

"No," the intern firmly said. "This port is not for sale." He pointed across the warehouse. "John was supposed to load a small pallet of vintage port from a different *quinta*, but he loaded newer port in error."

"The carbon 14 analysis detected the anomaly," Barb said.

Concerned that Barb would start another lecture, Adelle urged the intern to continue.

"Instead of owning up to his mistake, John hoped it would go away on its own." The intern sighed. "When the insurance company asked me to help with the investigation, I discovered his involvement." His eyes pleaded with Barb. "I was going to explain John's mistake to you here last week before we went on stage," he said.

"On stage?" Adelle asked. She was confused.

The intern held up his mandolin. "I play in the band on weekends to earn spending money. I saw Barb come in late, so I nodded to John to keep her company, but she left before we were done the first set."

Barb put her hands on her hips and glared at John.

"Why did you tell me the port was shipped from Lisbon?"

The intern groaned. "He didn't tell me that."

"It seemed like a good idea at the time," John mumbled, looking down at his feet.

Adelle had questions of her own. "Why did Manuel give us a bottle of this port?" she asked.

Again, the intern looked surprised and turned to his brother. After another rapid exchange of Portuguese, he turned back to Adelle and Barb. "Manuel is our cousin. My brother asked him to explain his mistake to you."

"Or were you trying to bribe us to drop the investigation?" Barb asked John.

"No," said John, alarmed. "The port was a peace offering, not a bribe. Manuel was supposed to make everything better."

"Then why didn't he tell us about your mistake?" Barb demanded.

John scowled. "Manuel said you wouldn't understand."

Adelle struggled not to grin as Barb got a taste of her own medicine.

"Why not?" Barb asked.

It was John's turn to glare at Barb. "Because you gulped down our family port in one quick swallow."

Guilty as charged. It was Adelle's turn to look at her feet in embarrassment. The serving was so small that she and Barb had assumed it was a shooter. She blushed. They had insulted Manuel by slamming back his family's precious port.

"It was truly amazing port," Adelle said, trying to defuse the situation. "You must be very proud."

John stood taller and grinned.

"Your cousin should have helped you by helping us," Barb said, uncrossing her arms.

John looked down at his feet again. "He did. Manuel said he warned you not to cause problems."

The intern briefly closed his eyes and shook his head. "What did he say?"

"*Nao partir a loica toda*," Adelle replied. It wasn't the only warning directed at them. "What about the baker in Favaios?"

"She is our aunt," John mumbled. "Manuel's mother."

Adelle rolled her eyes. Did the entire Duoro community know how naïve she and Barb had been about the family vintage port?

The intern turned to Barb. "When you texted that the investigation was going into recovery mode, I insisted John drive to Salamanca to tell you the truth."

Another piece of the puzzle clicked into place for Adelle. Bumping into John was not a coincidence. Barb had asked the intern where to get business cards.

"I started to tell you," John said, stuffing his hands in his pockets.

"All you said was to be careful not to buy port from strangers," Barb said crossly.

"Because the bottles sometimes get mixed up," John said in his defense. "I tried, but then you left."

"Because Adelle was motioning for me to join her."

Although Adelle felt bad, she suddenly craved chocolate.

The intern clapped John on his shoulder. "Like me, my brother tried to make things right," he said. "John is a good man. His biggest faults are avoiding conflicts and hoping problems go away on their own."

Adelle knew the feeling.

"Still, he's my brother, and I love him." The intern grinned. "John's going to be a father!"

"Which reminds me," Adelle said. "John, why did your wife phone and threaten me?" She told the men about the angry call in Portuguese.

Barb looked at her and pursed her lips. "What about 'I need to know what you know?'"

"I'm sorry," Adelle whispered as the brothers talked in rapid Portuguese. "I'll explain later."

The intern turned to Barb. "The business card taped to the top of the box fell off when you crossed the square. John picked it up and put it in his pocket. His wife found it there when she was doing the laundry. She thought he was having an affair." He chuckled. "With Junior."

Will this humiliation ever end?

Adelle finally understood what had happened. John's wife wanted "Junior" to get lost and leave her spouse and family alone.

"None of this makes sense," the intern said. "I don't know why the insurance company is investigating such a small claim."

Barb's eyes narrowed. "You call a seven-figure claim small?"

"Seven figures?" the intern exclaimed, eyes opening wide. He had another animated conversation with John before turning back to Barb. "How could twenty-four bottles of port be worth seven figures?"

"The bill-of-lading says twenty-four *barrels*," Barb replied, whipping her phone out of her pocket to show them.

"How many bottles are there in a barrel?" Adelle asked John.

"250," he replied.

Something didn't make sense. How could twenty-four barrels fit on one small pallet? Adelle asked Barb to make the bill-of-lading larger on the screen. Using the zoom feature, she found what she was looking for and handed the phone back to Barb. "Under quantity, it says '24 B.'"

"B for barrels," Barb said.

"No," John exclaimed. "B for bottles."

Barb twirled a strand of loose hair. "Then why is the claim for seven figures?" she demanded.

Adelle had an idea. "Is it possible that the distributor sensed an opportunity and submitted a fraudulent claim?"

Barb pursed her lips. "Exactly what I was thinking." She turned to the intern.

"If John can prove that only twenty-four bottles were shipped, we can confront the claimant."

"The shipper/receiver also plays in the band," the

intern said, looking at the time, then turning to leave. "We will get that for you after our next set."

Adelle woke the next morning to the heavenly aroma of fresh-brewed coffee. Opening one eye, she saw Barb sitting on the bed beside her, holding two steaming cups. "Good morning," she said brightly, handing one to Adelle.

As they relived the events from the night before, Adelle had a new appreciation for Barb.

"That was kind of you to give John and his wife the blanket you crocheted for your mom," Adelle said.

Barb smiled. "I'll have time to crochet another blue and white one on the flight home."

While the band played their last set the evening before, Barb had hurried back to the ship. She returned with the blanket and Tilly and Debbie, who were flushed with victory after winning the trivia contest.

"When Amelia asked how many private balconies looked over the Plaza Mayor square, Tilly knew the answer off by heart," Debbie had said, toasting her sister proudly.

"That's because I pay attention '24/7'," Tilly had explained.

Adelle was impressed. Tilly had proved that when she really wanted to remember something, she could. *Another lesson, Adelle.*

Adelle sipped her coffee. "How did your call go this

morning?" The previous evening, Barb and the intern had arranged an early morning conference call with the insurance company. "Did John and his brother get in trouble?"

"No," Barb replied. "The call went very well. We stuck to the relevant facts on a need-to-know basis. Twenty-four bottles were shipped. Not twenty-four barrels, as claimed by the distributor."

Adelle was relieved. She had become quite fond of John and his wife.

Barb set her coffee down and studied Adelle. "We need to debrief about the threatening call."

Adelle had been dreading the conversation. She reminded herself that she was done with avoiding confrontation. "I was afraid you would call me a drama queen again."

To her credit, Barb apologized. "But no more shrieking," she said, eyes twinkling. She pointed to a small box sitting on Adelle's bed. "Before you open that, I want to thank you for your bravery and diligence. I should call you Amelia."

"What do you mean?"

"You conquered your fear of the unknown and followed John into the warehouse. Then you discovered where I had made the wrong assumption about barrels versus bottles being shipped."

Adelle didn't know what to say.

"It's not the first time you've helped solve the case," Barb continued. "Thank you for your help on our previous river cruises, as well."

Adelle blushed. Until that moment, she hadn't real-ized how much she needed Barb's acknowledgment of her efforts. "Thank you," she said.

"During our call this morning, the intern spoke very highly of you. The insurance company was very impressed with our work and wants to engage us for another investigation."

Adelle looked up hopefully. "Us?"

Barb reached out and handed Adelle the box. "If you accept these, then yes, us."

Adelle opened the box and read her new business cards. She had been promoted to Senior Associate. "Affirmative!" she shrieked.

"Is Barb still working?" Debbie asked as Adelle joined the sisters for lunch before disembarking for their flights home.

"She'll be here soon," Adelle replied. "She has a lot of luggage to pack."

Debbie and Tilly had enjoyed shopping earlier that morning at the vendor tables set up along the Duoro.

"The early bird gets the worm," Tilly said, describing the one-of-a-kind lace tablecloth she had bought.

"We did pretty well for two old birds," Debbie quipped, launching into a description of her own purchases.

Adelle didn't want to talk anymore about shopping.

She had achieved her goal of being promoted. There was still one goal left. She lightly kicked Debbie under the table and winked. Debbie winked back.

"Sis, I'm not sure if you'll ever need another fundraising idea," Debbie began, "but if you do, I think you should have a pot party."

Tilly turned to Adelle and rolled her eyes. "See what I mean?"

Adelle laughed. "Give her a chance."

Debbie suggested that Tilly's group of town girl-friends could get together and sell potted plants in the spring. "Over the winter, the men can make planters from used pallets, you and your friends can pot them, and students can help promote them online."

Adelle held her breath. She and Debbie had worked out a plan that depended on Tilly's response. If she didn't like the idea, Debbie would admit that it came from Adelle. After all, the girls knew Adelle wasn't attached to her ideas; she would simply come up with another one.

"That's a good idea, Sis," Tilly finally said before turning to Adelle, eyebrow raised. "You need to come and visit me sometime."

Adelle grinned. How could life get any better?

Barb arrived just as the server brought the menus. Before she ordered, she looked at Tilly. "Do you drink Scotch?"

"Of course," Tilly replied. "Scotch is good for you."

"Our ancestors came from the Orkneys," Debbie said. "They drank it all the time."

Barb winked at Adelle. "Good. Are you girls inter-
ested in a cruise around the British Isles?"

**When Adelle and her friends investigate suspicious
cases while cruising the British Isles, will their
relentless pursuit of justice uncover the truth before
more victims get hurt?**

If you are enjoying the ebook, read ***Baffled in the
British Isles*** to find out. If you are enjoying the
paperback book, please scan the code below with your
phone or visit amazon.com/author/cheryldougan to buy
Baffled in the British Isles.

JOIN THE NEWSLETTER

GET ONBOARD!

Want to learn more about me, my characters, and upcoming releases and sales?

In the ebook, click to join my newsletter. If reading the paperback, visit tinyurl.com/cheryldouganbooks, or scan the code below with your phone to sign up!

www.cheryldouganauthor.com

You can also follow me on Amazon!

Visit <u>amazon.com/author/cheryldougan</u> or scan the code below with your phone.

GOOD KARMA

Thank you for reading my book. I hope you love Adelle and her friends as much as I do! If you could take a moment to leave a review, it would help other readers to discover the book, and your support and feedback would mean the world to me.

You can find all my books at amazon.com/author/cheryldougan or scan the code below with your phone.

THE RIVER CRUISE COZIES

Join Adelle as she meets new friends on a European river cruise. After they unravel the puzzle of missing diamonds together, they continue their adventures, exploring new destinations and solving mysteries along the way. Get ready for a delightful blend of friendship, adventure, and mystery, one river cruise at a time!

THE OCEAN CRUISE COZIES

Join Adelle and her friends on more fun adventures as she embraces her new role as a Senior Associate investigator. Follow along as they sail from one intriguing case to the next, navigating a world of friendship and intrigue in their relentless pursuit of justice.

ABOUT THE AUTHOR

Cheryl has always loved travel, meeting people, and storytelling. She enjoys writing light-hearted cozy mysteries featuring the same quirky cast of characters as they solve mysteries together.

When she is not writing, reading, or planning her next trip, Cheryl enjoys being outdoors, listening to her characters as they get excited about their next escapade.

Find Cheryl online at: **www.cheryldouganauthor.com**

Printed in Great Britain
by Amazon